KU-743-050

# Cockerel's
# Big Egg

First published in 2004 by
Franklin Watts
96 Leonard Street
London
EC2A 4XD

Franklin Watts Australia
45–51 Huntley Street
Alexandria
NSW 2015

Text © Damian Harvey 2004
Illustration © François Hall 2004

A CIP catalogue record for this book is available
from the British Library.

ISBN 0 7496 5729 4 (hbk)
ISBN 0 7496 5767 7 (pbk)

**Series Editor:** Jackie Hamley
**Series Advisor:** Dr Barrie Wade
**Cover Design:** Jason Anscomb
**Design:** Peter Scoulding

Printed in Hong Kong / China

# Cockerel's
# Big Egg

by Damian Harvey and François Hall

W
FRANKLIN WATTS
LONDON•SYDNEY

The farmyard is always busy.

The chickens need feeding.

The cows need milking.

The sheep need taking to the fields.

"It's too busy!" cried the Farmer.

"Something will HAVE to go!"

"Did you hear that?" clucked the Chickens. "Something has to go! But it won't be us, because we give eggs for the Farmer's breakfast."

8

9

"It won't be me," miaowed Cat.
"I chase the rats."

"Or me," baaed Sheep. "I give
wool for his clothes."

"It won't be me," mooed Cow.
"I give milk."

Everyone looked at Cockerel.

"I wake the Farmer up,"
crowed Cockerel.

But Cat shook her head. "The
Farmer's clock wakes him up."

13

The Chickens laughed.

"You stupid Cockerel – thinking you woke the Farmer."

"Well, I crow and bring up the sun," crowed Cockerel.

14

But Cow shook *her* head.

"Sometimes the sun comes up

before you crow."

"You stupid Cockerel," clucked the Chickens, "thinking you brought up the sun!"
Cockerel hung his head.

17

Then Cat spoke again. "Cockerel makes sure you Chickens lay lots of eggs."

"RIDICULOUS!" laughed the Chickens, louder than before. "You must be as stupid as that Cockerel!"

19

But Cat told everyone that Cockerel could lay an egg big enough to feed the Farmer and all his family.

"And what would happen to you Chickens then?" miaowed Cat. "Chicken dinner, that's what!"

"Nonsense!" clucked the Chickens.
"Everyone knows that cockerels
can't lay eggs."

"Very well," miaowed Cat.

"We'll have a Big Egg
competition. If Cockerel wins, you
Chickens must stay in the shed to
make room in the farmyard."

"But I can't lay eggs," clucked Cockerel. "Ssshhh!" purred Cat and whispered his plan.

That night Cockerel and Cat crept into the shed. "COCK-A-DOODLE-DOO!" crowed Cockerel.

The Chickens jumped out of their nests in surprise.

"It's time to see who has laid the biggest egg," miaowed Cat.

Everyone looked at the Chickens'
eggs. Then they went outside to see
Cockerel's egg.

And there, in the
middle of the pond,
was the biggest egg
they had ever seen.
They could hardly
believe their eyes.
Cockerel
had won!

29

The next morning, the giant egg had gone. But the Chickens stayed in the shed as they had promised.

So they never saw the Farmer take away the old tractor to make more room in the farmyard!

Hopscotch has been specially designed to fit the requirements of the National Literacy Strategy. It offers real books by top authors and illustrators for children developing their reading skills.

## There are 21 Hopscotch stories to choose from:

**Marvin, the Blue Pig**
Written by Karen Wallace
Illustrated by Lisa Williams

**Plip and Plop**
Written by Penny Dolan
Illustrated by Lisa Smith

**The Queen's Dragon**
Written by Anne Cassidy
Illustrated by Gwyneth Williamson

**Flora McQuack**
Written by Penny Dolan
Illustrated by Kay Widdowson

**Willie the Whale**
Written by Joy Oades
Illustrated by Barbara Vagnozzi

**Naughty Nancy**
Written by Anne Cassidy
Illustrated by Desideria Guicciardini

**Run!**
Written by Sue Ferraby
Illustrated by Fabiano Fiorin

**The Playground Snake**
Written by Brian Moses
Illustrated by David Mostyn

**"Sausages!"**
Written by Anne Adeney
Illustrated by Roger Fereday

**The Truth about Hansel and Gretel**
Written by Karina Law
Illustrated by Elke Counsell

**Pippin's Big Jump**
Written by Hilary Robinson
Illustrated by Sarah Warburton

**Whose Birthday Is It?**
Written by Sherryl Clark
Illustrated by Jan Smith

**The Princess and the Frog**
Written by Margaret Nash
Illustrated by Martin Remphry

**Flynn Flies High**
Written by Hilary Robinson
Illustrated by Tim Archbold

**Clever Cat**
Written by Karen Wallace
Illustrated by Anni Axworthy

**Moo!**
Written by Penny Dolan
Illustrated by Melanie Sharp

**Izzie's Idea**
Written by Jillian Powell
Illustrated by Leonie Shearing

**Roly-poly Rice Ball**
Written by Penny Dolan
Illustrated by Diana Mayo

**I Can't Stand It!**
Written by Anne Adeney
Illustrated by Mike Phillips

**Cockerel's Big Egg**
Written by Damian Harvey
Illustrated by François Hall

**The Truth about those Billy Goats**
Written by Karina Law
Illustrated by Graham Philpot